For Jack, Olivia, Cleo, Gillian, Kalen & Tripton
and
Lachlan, Tate & Macdonald

May all children be loved and cared for.

Nana-Hugs-a-Lot

by Sandra Hazlett

Illustrated by Ann Kuckelman Cobb

This is our Nana.
She loves hugs.
We think her
hugs are her
way of talking.

Nana always greets us with a big HELLO HUG. She is so glad to see us!

GOOD MORNING
HUGS are a
snuggly start
to the day.

Our SQUEEZE
TIGHT HUGS
with Nana make
us giggle
and laugh.

READING
TOGETHER HUGS
take us to far
away places.

HANG IN THERE!
HUGS help us
keep trying
when things get
hard.

GOOD JOB!
HUGS
make us proud
we did it!

I AM SORRY
YOU ARE SAD
HUGS help the
hurt go away.

GOOD NIGHT
HUGS make the
dark safe and
dreams sweet.

GOODBYE HUGS
say thank you,
we will be back
soon.

Yes, our Nana's hugs are her way of talking. And she talks a lot!

We think we'll
call her

NANA-HUGS-A-LOT!

Ann Kuckelman Cobb is an artist and anthropologist. In her years of learning and teaching anthropology, she became fascinated by the wonderful stories of how people of various cultures believed the world came to be and how it continued to function with the help of a vast array of spirit beings, animal helpers and shamans. Drawing on these stories, she wrote and illustrated two children's books, **Creation Stories and Other Tales from Near and Far**, and **Three Stories for Lachlan**. Her illustrations for **Nana-Hugs-a-Lot** continue Ann's interest in how children see the world and how the language of hugs can convey warmth and caring for children of all ages.

annkcobb@gmail.com

One of Sandra's favorite memories in the course of raising three children is her seven year stint as the Story Hour Mom every Thursday morning in her youngest son's school library. For three hours she read to the children in preschool though first grade books from her own childrens' library as well as those available at school. When grandchildren started to visit at her house she already had a long list of "must reads" and an even longer list of ideas for new books. She believes that helping young children develop a love of books is a particular joy of grand parenthood.

Made in the USA
Coppell, TX
27 July 2021